ANTS LOVE PICNICS TOO

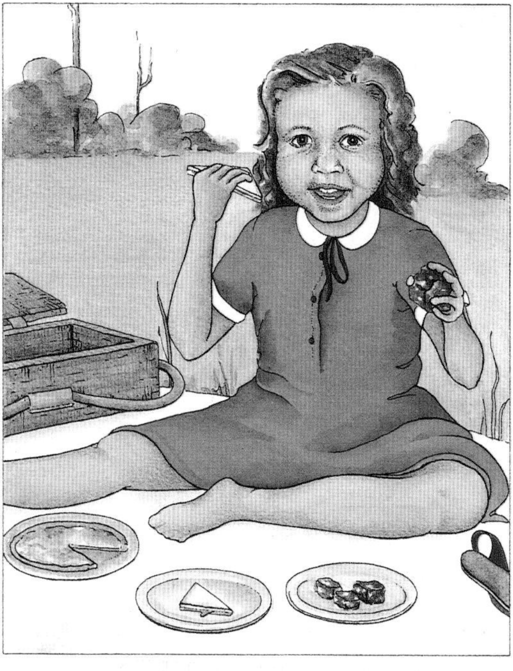

D0061980

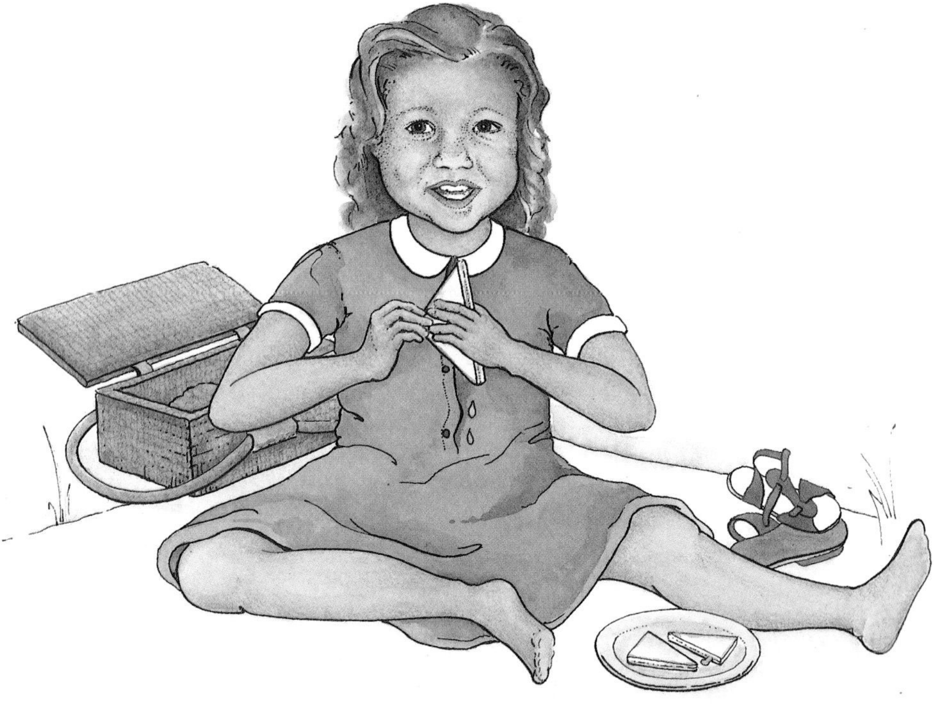

I love honey sandwiches.

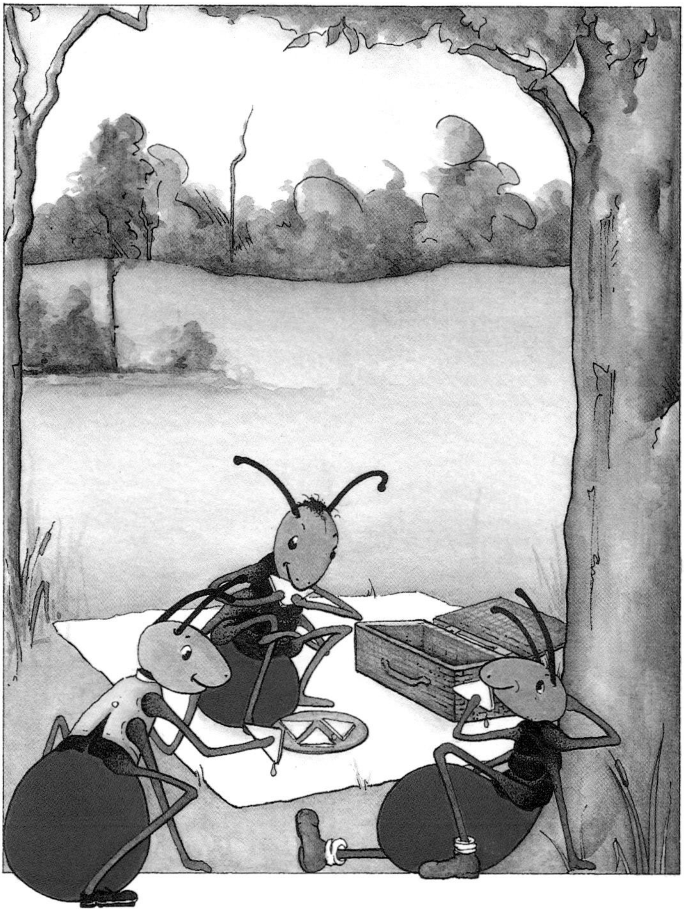

Ants do too.

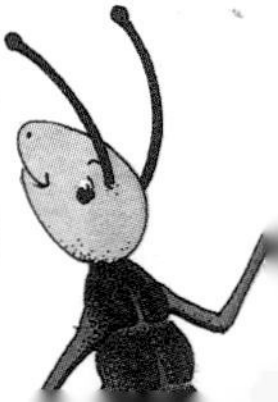

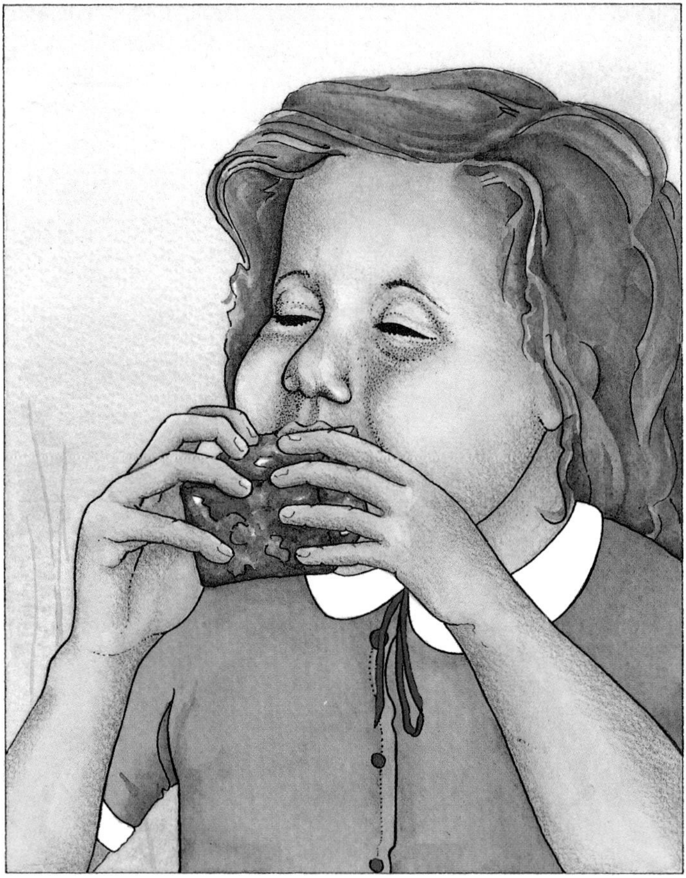

I love chocolate brownies.

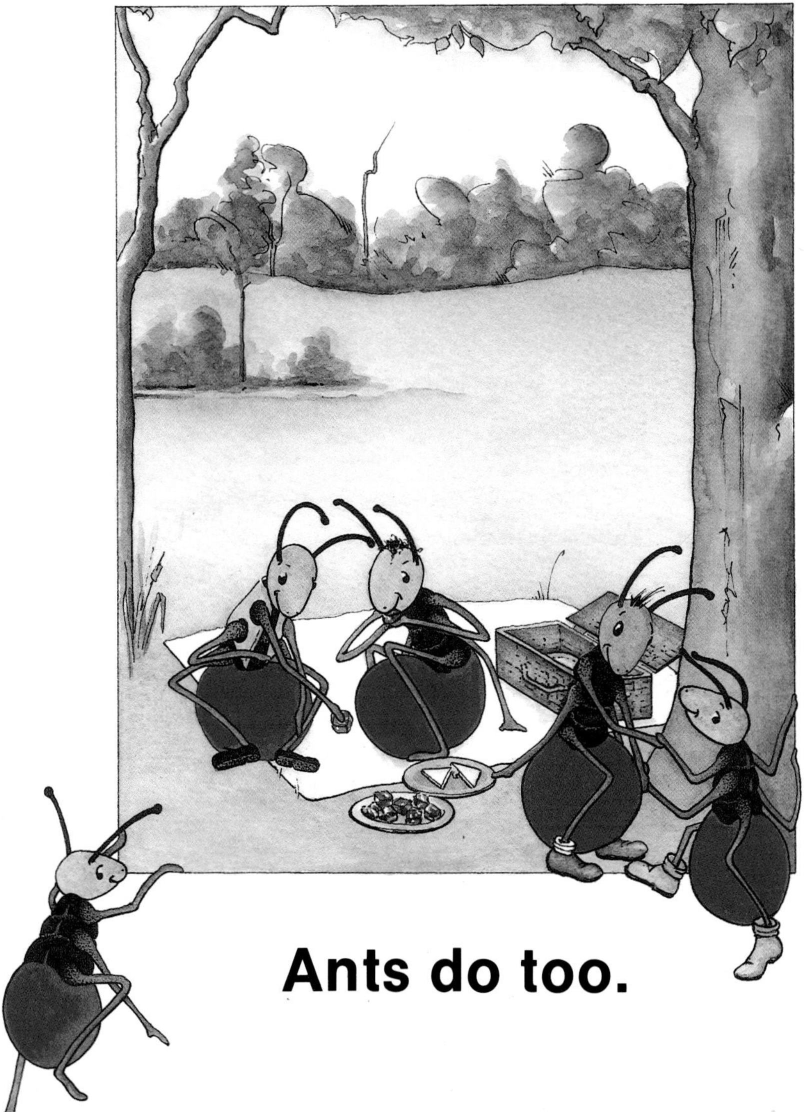

Ants do too.

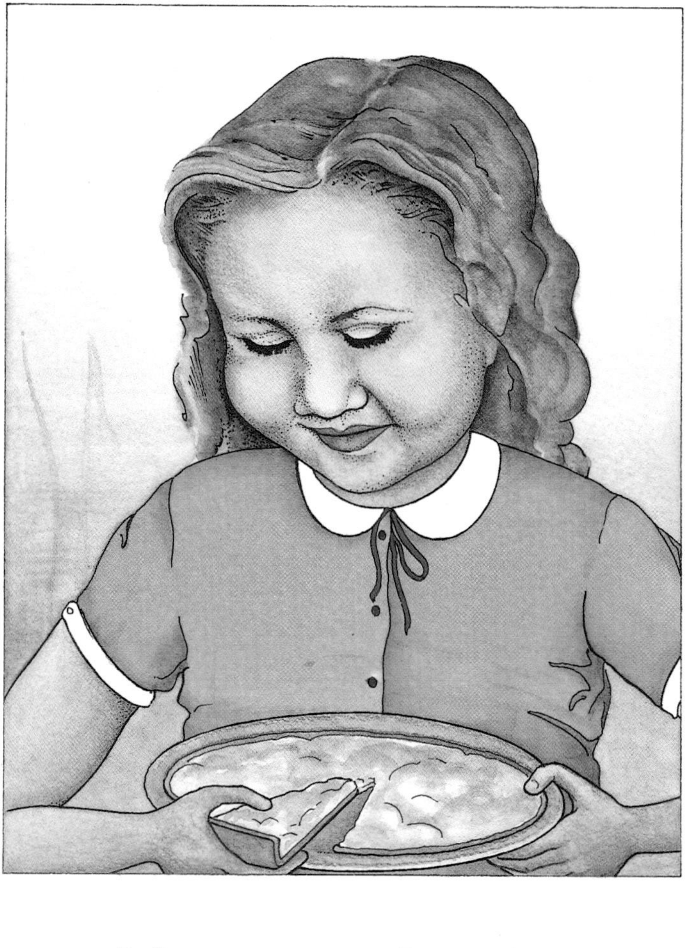

I love apple pie.

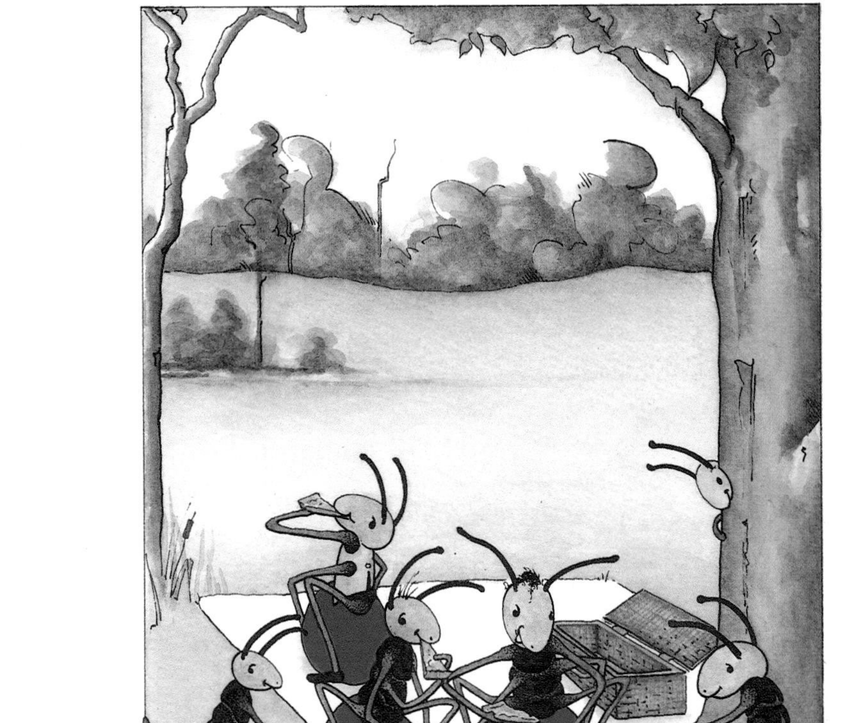

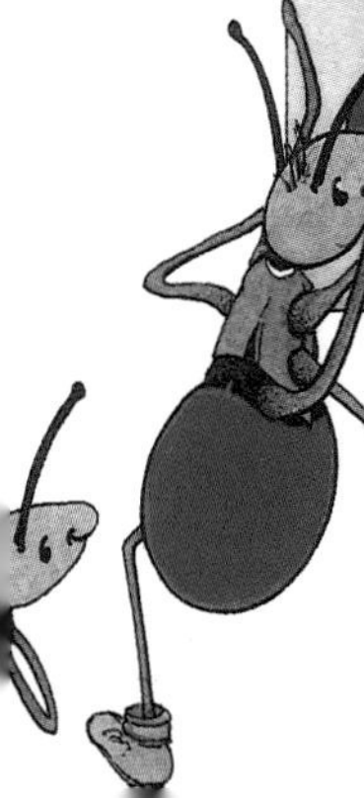

Ants do too.

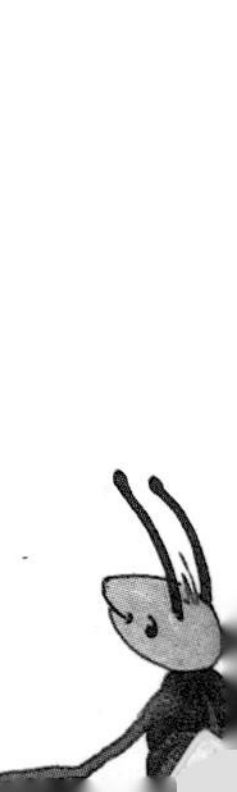

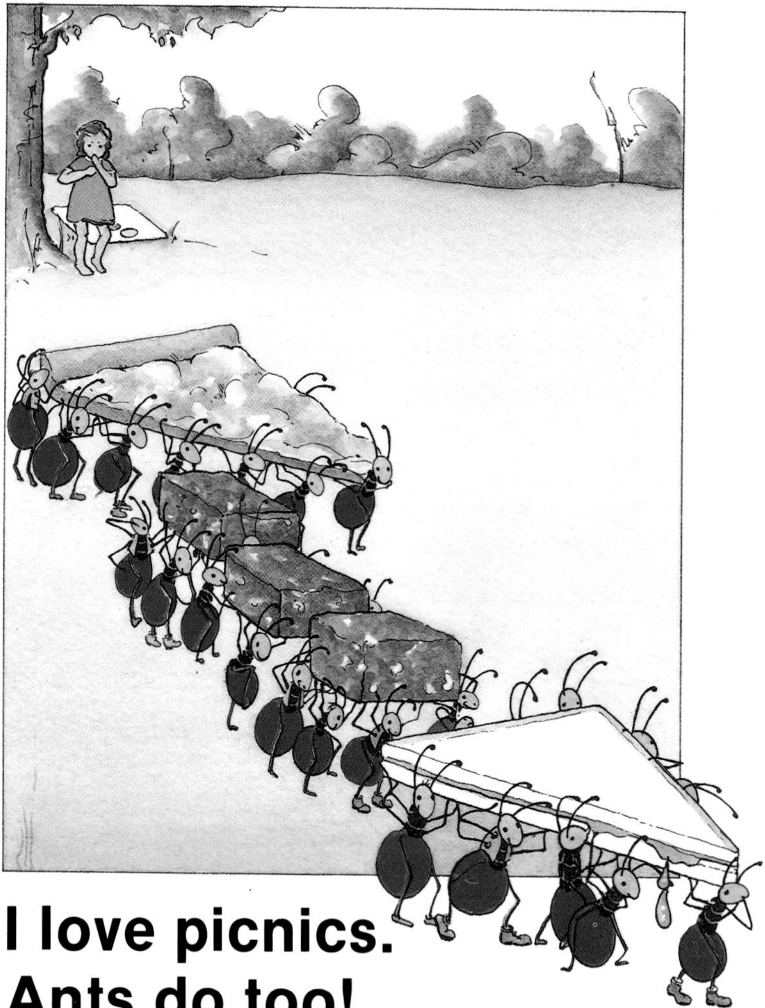

I love picnics.
Ants do too!